Dear Reader,

Welcome to the latest edition of *The Zoological Times*, packed as ever with news, features and interviews – and plenty of food, if you like eating paper (I'm looking at you, cockroaches and book lice)! These are tricky times for our planet, and in this issue we focus on some of the threats facing the animal kingdom as the Earth heats up. The animal kingdom is huge, and we're all very different, but whether we live on land or in water, soar in the air or burrow underground, we all understand how important it is to protect the world we live in. Human beings do need to be reminded sometimes, though – those mammals have been nothing but trouble since they discovered fire! But it's not all doom and gloom. Get the low-down on the animal Olympics, get mane maintenance tips from the world's leading lion hairstylists and test your brains with puzzles and quizzes! Unless you're a sea sponge and don't have a brain. BUT FIRST: why not turn to page 32 and find out what animal you actually are?!

Happy reading!

Aileen

Aileen Aye-aye, editor

Text and illustrations
© The Quarto Group 2018
Photographs © The Trustees of the
Natural History Museum, London 2018

Written by Stella Gurney
Illustrated by Matthew Hodson

First Published in 2018 by
Lincoln Children's Books,
an imprint of The Quarto Group.
The Old Brewery, 6 Blundell Street,
London N7 9BH, United Kingdom.
T (0)20 7700 6700 F (0)20 7700 8066
www.QuartoKnows.com
Published in association with the
Natural History Museum, London

All rights reserved.
A catalogue record for this book is
available from the British Library.

ISBN 978-1-84780-920-9

Illustrated with mixed media
Set in Chaparral Pro

Published by Jenny Broom
and Rachel Williams
Designed by Nicola Price
Edited by Kate Davies
Production by Jenny Cundill
and Kate O'Riordan

Manufactured in Dongguan, China
TL112017

9 8 7 6 5 4 3 2 1

CONTENTS

NEWS

THE BIG WARM: CAUSE UNCOVERED

New evidence is emerging about the causes of the Big Warm. The world is getting hotter, there's no doubt about it. Maybe you're thinking, "Ooh, great, I could do with a suntan." But trust us, this is not a good thing. Ice is melting, deserts are spreading – and our fellow animals are suffering.

PET DETECTIVES

It has been suspected for some time that global warming is down to human beings, since only they hold the secret to fire. Reports confirming this have been coming in from animals all over the world who live with humans as "pets". "I'll admit, I like a snooze by the fire," said Snookums from the UK. "But my human even heats her house in summer – then leaves the windows open!". Diddums from the USA claimed, "My human collects her children from school every day in her car and waits for them with the engine running. I'd prefer the walk – and frankly, she could do with it!"

SHOCKING

However, the reports also claim that many humans *know* they are the cause of the Big Warm – and are doing little about it. Pigeons allege that human newspapers are full of news about

Pigeon perusing paper panics at planetary peril

> **"My human even heats her house in summer – then leaves the windows open!"**

what they call the "environmental crisis". "It would appear that many humans simply don't care about global warming," agrees Eli Elephant, head of the Animal Committee. "Others refuse to believe it's their fault – they think the Earth just started heating up of its own accord. Either way, they really should address the problem, since it will affect them as much as the rest of us."

LOSING YOUR COLOUR?

FEATHERS FADING?

Flamingos: you really are what you eat! The deep oranges, reds and pinks of your feathers come from a chemical in the molluscs and crustaceans you munch for lunch. But when those are in short supply, your feathers can appear grey and dull. If this problem is affecting you, look no further. You need:

IN THE PINK

A new supplement that'll brighten you up in no time.
In the pink: you'll be tickled pink!

CAMEL GETS THE HUMP

Camels are almost extinct in the wild, but lots of them still exist – because they are useful to humans. For thousands of years, camels have carried heavy loads, receiving food and drink in return. There are only 1,000 wild Bactrian camels (with two humps) left, and wild dromedary camels (with one hump) no longer exist at all – though there are lots of feral ones around. But domesticated (tame) camels can be found all over the world. We asked Barry Bactrian the question on everyone's minds: what's in those humps? "A supply of fat I use when I'm hungry," Barry huffed. "Not that it's any of your business."

POLAR BEARS: ON THIN ICE

With the Big Warm comes the Big Melt – the amount of ice in the Arctic is getting smaller as temperatures get higher. What does this mean for the polar bears that live there? Pam Polar Bear gives us the inside scoop.

Polar bears: much less cheerful than they used to be

"We hunt seals during the winter, out on the ice," says Pam. "But there aren't as many of them these days. The ice isn't around for as long as it used to be, either, and when it is, there's less of it, so we have to swim longer from land to reach it. My cousin swam for nine days solid last year before she reached ice – she nearly didn't make it. We've all lost weight, and we don't have as many cubs as we used to. I don't know what's going to happen to us."

But there is hope: if humans use more sustainable sources of energy like wind and solar power, burn fewer fossil fuels and recycle more, they could stop the planet getting hotter. So lobby your local human today!

COMPETITION CORNER

It's competition time! Just complete the quizzes and questions on every page and send your answers in via pigeon post to win a year's worth of free food* for you and your family!

*As long as you like eating aphids

TARSIER
PROFILE

LENGTH: 9.5–14 cm
WEIGHT: 102–130 g

APPEARANCE: Tarsiers look like two huge brown marbles surrounded by fur and feet. Their eyes are MASSIVE. They're cute!

HABITAT: If you're looking for a tarsier, look up. You'll find it clinging onto a tree in the islands and rainforests of South East Asia.

DIET: Tarsiers are the only completely meat-eating primate. They eat insects, birds, frogs… whatever they can get their hands on. Don't look so cute now, do they?

CONSERVATION STATUS: Endangered! Their trees are being chopped down and they're in serious danger of becoming extinct.

BEHAVIOUR: They're most active at night, when they hunt. Their massive eyes and excellent hearing means they can locate their prey easily.

TOP FACT: Tarsiers can turn their heads 180 degrees to look behind them. Amazing!

HIPPOPOTAMUS
PROFILE

LENGTH: 3–5 m
WEIGHT: 1,400–4,500 kg

● **APPEARANCE:** With their big, blunt snouts, tiny ears and round bellies, hippos look harmless and a little bit silly. They're also huge – the third-largest land mammals after elephants and rhinoceros.

✛ **HABITAT:** African countries south of the Sahara desert. They need to spend lots of time in the water or their skin gets dry and cracked, so they live in areas with rivers and lakes.

● **DIET:** Mostly grass – 35 kg of it a night, in fact. That's roughly the weight of a ten-year-old human.

♥ **CONSERVATION STATUS:** Vulnerable. Humans are gradually pushing hippos out of their habitat – and they're are hunted for their meat, too.

❻ **BEHAVIOUR:** Stroppy! Hippos are NOT harmless and silly – they're extremely dangerous and kill around 3,000 humans a year (compared to sharks, which kill around 5). Hippos are vegetarian though, so at least they won't eat you after they've killed you. They chill out in water in the day and come out to eat at night.

❓ **TOP FACT:** Hippos live mostly in water, but they can't swim or float – they stand on the ground beneath the surface. If you see a hippo open its mouth, run – it's not yawning, it's about to attack.

❶ ## SPOT THE ODD ONE OUT

One of these ladybirds is different from the rest. Can you find the odd one out?

"WE'RE NOT FISH!" SAY ANIMALS THAT LOOK LIKE FISH

Angry whales and dolphins gathered outside the Animal Committee yesterday to protest because they are often confused for fish. "We're mammals and proud," explained Denise Dolphin. "Just like all those furry creatures that get so much attention – lions and pigs and humans and that lot."

"We're mammals and proud, just like all those furry creatures that get so much attention"

NO EGGS

"We have backbones, warm blood, and we give birth to live babies rather than eggs – what more do they want?" said Wilma Whale, who was completely blocking the entrance to the Committee building. "Everyone knows that fish are cold blooded. Plus they lay eggs – loads of them! They're nothing like us. We're sick of people getting it wrong."

CREEPY

The ocean-going mammals were joined in their protest by a group of spiders, crabs, centipedes and millipedes.

A group of flamingos chat after eating protesters yesterday

"We're all part of a big group of creatures called arthropods. Cressida, that crab over there, is related to us, too. She's a crustacean. Aren't you Cressida? Wait – where's she gone?" But Cressida didn't reply, because she was busy being eaten by a flamingo.

BIRD

"I suppose we're lucky," mused Fatima Flamingo, after munching a few more protesters. "Everyone knows what a bird is. Wings, feathers, backbones, that sort of thing. Same for reptiles – everyone recognizes a lizard – and amphibians. You know where you are with a frog. It must be harder for the squishy creatures that no one knows what to do with, like snails. Bet they don't get invited to many parties."

"We get invited to plenty of parties!" said Sybil Snail, getting quite angry – and there's nothing worse than an angry snail. "I'm part of the mollusc family, and I'm always being invited to tea with slugs, or underwater discos with squid and octopuses. I don't tend to go to those, though, because of the drowning."

At that point, Eli Elephant squeezed out of the building to separate the squabbling animals and said, "Let's remember that whatever kind of animal we are, we're all related."

> "Let's remember that whatever kind of animal we are, we're all related."

"We know exactly how the whales and dolphins feel," said Tara Tarantula. "People are always getting us mixed up with insects. It really isn't hard to get it right. Sure, we're all invertebrates (we don't have backbones) and our bodies are divided into segments. But insects have got six legs and spiders have got eight."

"We are cousins, though," pointed out Myra Millipede.

❷ WHO IS THIS?

This creature appears in the article above – but who is it? Join the dots to find out!

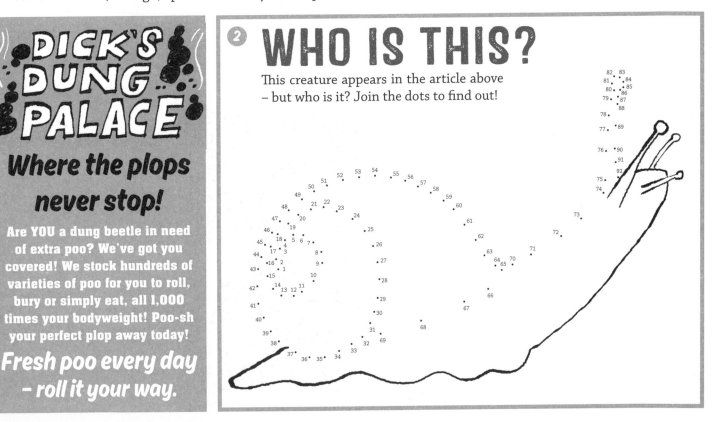

THE BRUISE NEWS!

"Gerroff!" yells giraffe

For all their large, mournful eyes and spindly looking legs, giraffes can be vicious so-and-sos if the mood takes them. And it certainly took Gerry and Geoff last Wednesday as they tussled on the savannah in Chad, central Africa. The reason? They were necking (fighting), trying to prove who was the biggest and strongest. Our reporter has the lowdown.

HINDQUARTERS

"We could tell trouble was brewing as soon as Gerry appeared," said Germaine, an eyewitness. "He sidled up as Geoff was nibbling at a tree and gave him a shove with his hindquarters. Geoff sort of stumbled, but he wasn't going to back down, no way. He swung his neck at Gerry, but Gerry was too quick for him. Geoff's much older than Gerry. He probably thought 'Who's this cheeky pipsqueak?' We all thought the same at first – but Gerry soon showed us who's boss. You wouldn't want to run into him on a dark night."

NOWHERE

"Gerry just appeared from nowhere, like a lone ranger!" giggled another young eyewitness. "He'd been out on the plains on his own, like lots of the bulls [that's "males" for all the non-giraffes out there], but he must have decided it was time to join a herd. And he had to get Geoff out of the way first!"

> "Usually when two giraffes fight, one of 'em backs down"

"THUNK"

The fight lasted about ten minutes, with both giraffes taking great swipes at each other with their necks. Huge thunks could be heard and dust clouds were raised as they each swung their necks to the side and then back into their rival's body. The results were quite shocking.

SHOCKING

"Usually when two giraffes fight, one of 'em backs down," said Germaine. "But not these two. They went at it for ages, bish bash bosh, until poor old Geoff just collapsed and lay there, knocked out. When he finally came to, he limped off into the sunset to live by himself on the plains for a bit – he won't be able to show his face here again, not with Gerry around."

FATHER DEFENDS SON IN PREDATOR FACE-OFF

REGGIE REINDEER HAS A MAGNIFICENT SET OF ANTLERS – THANK GOODNESS!

He needed them the other day when he saw his young calf, Richard, about to be attacked by a brown bear near the Norwegian border. Reggie thought quickly and put himself between the bear and Richard, lowering his antlers, snorting and stamping the ground with his hooves in an effort to put the bear off. Fortunately, his quick thinking worked. He made himself seem so terrifying that the bear thought better of it and moved on. Nice one, Reggie!

"I didn't think twice – nobody hurts my Richard. He's got the cutest little baby face."

❸ MINI-MAZE

Help Reggie Reindeer reach his calf on the other side of the fir forest.

HONEY BADGER
PROFILE

LENGTH: 55–77 cm
WEIGHT: 5–16 kg

👁 **APPEARANCE:** A bit like a badger but with scarier teeth. The white stripe down its back earned it the badger name, though it's actually more of a weasel.

✛ **HABITAT:** Grasslands, mountains, forests and deserts in Africa, India and Western Asia.

🍎 **DIET:** These guys raid beehives for honey – they don't mind bee stings. They also eat eggs, berries and most animals smaller than them – rodents, frogs, birds and snakes (even venomous ones).

🖤 **CONSERVATION STATUS:** Fine. These little dudes are seriously tough – they have very few predators and can look after themselves, thank you very much.

🎵 **BEHAVIOUR:** Hardcore. Honey badgers will have a go at anyone and anything. Horse? No problem. Lion? Bring it on. Massive buffalo? It'll have you.

❓ **TOP FACT:** They smell disgusting. Like skunks, honey badgers release a stinky liquid. Apparently the smell is so "suffocating" that bees are almost knocked out by it, so the honey badger can nick all the honey while they're recovering.

❹ WHO IS THIS?

Join the dots to find out!

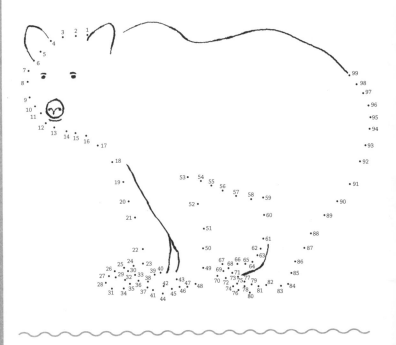

...AND FINALLY...

Leonard, Leslie and Lamar Lion were surprised last Thursday by an unusually bold cackle (group) of hyenas. Instead of prowling and waiting for the lions to eat their fill of the kill (a full-grown buffalo), the hyenas began an attack of their own, closing in on the lions and snapping at their tails. The lions, all young and inexperienced, appeared threatened, which was all the encouragement the hyenas needed. Cackling and howling, they called more of their clan to the scene, until at last, outnumbered, the lions backed off, leaving the buffalo for the hyenas to eat. When asked to comment, pride leader Lenny said, "This sort of thing never happened in my day. Those young lions should be ashamed of themselves. And just wait till I get my claws on those cackly little blighters!".

IN OTHER NEWS...

YOU'RE KIDDING
Mountain Goat Escapes Landslide

Idris Ibex said he was lucky to be alive after the ground he was standing on crumbled away yesterday. Ibex, a species of mountain goat, are well known for their climbing skills. They live high up in the craggy mountain ranges of Europe and regularly climb almost-sheer cliff faces, leaping more than three metres to the nearest tiny ledge or foothold. So it came as a shock to Idris Ibex when he found himself slip-sliding away! "It'd never happened to me before," he confessed. "My hooves are so well suited to climbing. They're hard but flexible and soft inside with separate 'toes', for gripping. They're also slightly hollow, so they almost sucker on to a surface. But if the surface *itself* comes away... well, you're in trouble!" Idris slid for several metres before he managed to leap to a nearby ledge, escaping the landslide. No other creatures were reported hurt.

Idris, back on solid ground

VAMPIRE CRÈCHE PRONOUNCED "OUTSTANDING"

A crèche operated by a community of vampire bats in Mexico has been declared "outstanding" after inspectors observed high levels of cooperation between members. The bats call each other "roostmates" and form strong friendships, helping each other out whenever they can. "We were really impressed," said an inspector. "Roostmates were grooming one another for fleas and looking after and even feeding each other's babies. Often, a bat who had been hunting would return and regurgitate blood for bats who had been left in the cave to babysit or because they were ill or too weak to fly. That's right – as their name suggests, vampire bats drink blood from mammals. They can't live without it for more than two days, so the guys sharing their food are literally life-savers." A community spokesbat said, "We're over the moon to get this rating! Not over the sun though, as we're nocturnal creatures!" Fortunately, the inspectors' rating is not affected by bad jokes.

⑤ CAN YOU SPOT WHAT COMES NEXT IN THE PATTERN?

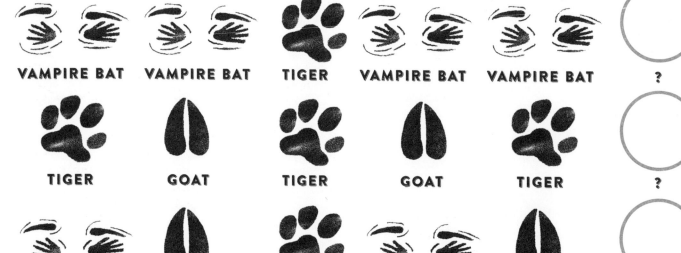

VAMPIRE BAT	VAMPIRE BAT	TIGER	VAMPIRE BAT	VAMPIRE BAT	?
TIGER	GOAT	TIGER	GOAT	TIGER	?
VAMPIRE BAT	GOAT	TIGER	VAMPIRE BAT	GOAT	?

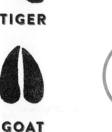

⑥ FLASH QUIZ!

(True) OR (False) ?

1. A male tiger and female lion produce a liger.

....

2. The Earth's magnetic pull runs from East to West.

....

3. Vampire bats don't really feed on blood, despite their name.

....

4. Okapis aren't very sociable animals.

....

5. Ibex goats can jump to heights of over three metres.

....

6. Vampire bats live alone.

....

"Lose the Ligers!"
Demands Tiger

A male tiger has called for a ban on interspecies mating. "Mating between male lions and female tigers means we have these massive great ligers about and they're bigger than all of us. It ain't right!" insists Terry, who isn't as concerned about mating between male tigers and lionesses because it produces tiglons, which are much smaller. We say chill out, Terry – ligers and tiglons are extremely rare, since tigers and lions generally don't share the same habitat.

Terry: "I hate lions. And I ain't lying."

OKAPI
PROFILE

HEIGHT: 1.5 m
WEIGHT: 200–350 kg

👁 **APPEARANCE:** Looks a bit like a zebra. Or a deer. Let's just say it's confused about its identity.

✛ **HABITAT:** The tropical forests of Central Africa.

🍎 **DIET:** These chaps eat grasses, trees, ferns, fruit and fungi – strictly vegetarian food only.

❤ **CONSERVATION STATUS:** Yup, you've guessed it – endangered. There are only about 25,000 in the wild.

☯ **BEHAVIOUR:** Okapis tend to hang out alone. They're shy and peaceful and keep their nose out of other people's business.

❓ **TOP FACT:** Okapis may look like zebras, but they're the only living relatives of the giraffe!

ANIMAL MAGNETISM

A steady stream of reports from all over the world suggests that the Earth's magnetism may be growing weaker. Many animals have an internal compass that senses the North/South pull of the Earth's natural magnetism. We use it to navigate when we're travelling for long distances without easily recognizable landmarks. It's the reason why large herds of mammals such as deer or cattle all face the same way when grazing, something which has puzzled humans for centuries (much to our amusement).

This isn't the first time the Earth's magnetism has dropped – it also occured hundreds of thousands of years ago, forcing many species to adopt different methods of navigation, before gradually growing stronger again. "There's no doubt the Earth's magnetism comes and goes," confirmed a spokeswolf from the Animal Committee, "but this is the first time for centuries it has dipped so low, so it pays to be prepared."

The Committee is organizing a series of workshops to teach creatures other ways of finding their way about. Looking at Landmarks and Star Sussing are the first. Find out more at your local watering hole.

TRADE & BUSINESS

SHARE REPORT

We are pleased to report that a healthy system of sharing and cooperation continues between species. For example, oxpecker birds eat annoying insects from the backs of giraffes, zebras or cattle, (see right), and rabbits kindly allow wheatear birds to nest in their burrows. And there is still almost no murder (i.e. killing apart from what is necessary for food) in the animal kingdom. That always makes the shareholders happy!

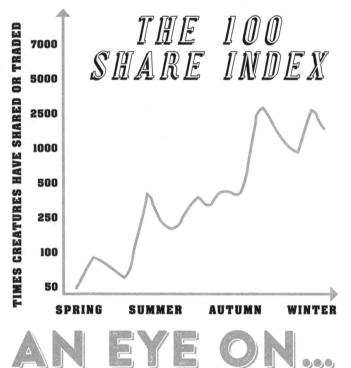

THE 100 SHARE INDEX

Y-axis: TIMES CREATURES HAVE SHARED OR TRADED — 7000, 5000, 2500, 1000, 500, 250, 100, 50

X-axis: SPRING, SUMMER, AUTUMN, WINTER

AN EYE ON...
the human exchange market

Human beings are an extraordinary species. They exchange small pieces of metal for food, shelter and even water. Some individuals gather lots of metal while others have none, and this lack of equality leads to some colonies being healthy and others malnourished. The metal pieces can also be stolen, which leads to violence and aggression between members of the species who will hurt each other to obtain it. It is an extraordinary and unique system that seems to bring little success to the species as a whole. Not a model to copy.

A HELPING BEAK

BY ZINEDINE ZEBRA

"Cleaning symbioses": we've all heard the phrase, but what does it actually mean? Well, it's the name for a deal that we see carried out often amongst different species in our kingdom: one gets a meal while the other gets a clean. Plover and sandpiper birds sometimes hop around the mouth of a crocodile, pecking out leeches and bits of food caught between the croc's teeth – yum! Oxpecker birds rummage around in zebras' fur for a tasty tick or two (thanks for that, oxpeckers!).

An alligator, trying to look friendly and get in on some teeth cleaning

And there is a whole group of fish known as "cleaner fish" who give larger sea creatures a full once-over, nibbling away at the tiny parasites living under their scales. It's a straight and simple swap: both sides get something out of it. Long live interspecies cooperation!

7 *See if you can unscramble this phrase*

GINRASH SI

_ _ _ _ _ _ _

RAGNIC

_ _ _ _ _ _

ZEBRA PROFILE

LENGTH: 2–2.6 m
WEIGHT: 350 kg

APPEARANCE: Zebras look like black-and-white stripy horses. You might think the jazzy stripes would make them stand out, but no – apparently the stripes play tricks on your eyes, making zebras harder to spot.

HABITAT: The plains, mountains and grasslands of Africa.

DIET: Greens, greens, greens!

CONSERVATION STATUS: Doing just fine or endangered, depending on the species.

BEHAVIOUR: Zebras believe in safety in numbers, so they hang out in herds. Often, these are groups of mums with their foals and one male who helps look after all the kids.

TOP FACT: No two zebras' stripes are the same – like human fingerprints, every single pattern is unique.

CHAIN REACTION EXPLAINED

BY PROFESSOR BATTY BATELEUR EAGLE

There is so much in our world that depends on a beautifully balanced system of "mutual benefit" – that is, everyone does their bit, and everyone gets what they need in exchange. Animals breathe in oxygen… and breathe out carbon dioxide. Plants "breathe in" carbon dioxide… and "breathe out" oxygen. It's magical! We're made for each other! Then there are food chains. You may not like vegetables, but still you need plants to grow so that the animals you snack on have something to eat. If the plants disappear, so will your snack. We all depend on each other, and the sooner some species understand that, the better. (Naming no names.) (Okay, humans.)

The partnership between a sea anemone and a hermit crab is a particularly touching one and often lasts for their entire lifetimes. These little guys eat together, grow together and even sometimes move together. Hermit crabs don't have their own shells, so they take empty ones that other creatures don't need any more. If crabby gets too big for his shell and needs to find a new one, anemone will go too! Or (get this), the anemone covers the bits of the crab that don't fit in the shell, so they don't have to move at all. Cute! If anything threatens Kermit the Hermit, Emily Anemone will be on the case, flashing her stinging tentacles to see off the bullies. A symbiotic relationship we could all learn from!

⑧ SPOT THE DIFFERENCE

Can you find six differences between these pictures?

SPOTLIGHT ON...

The weird and wonderful

Life wouldn't be much fun if we didn't have someone to point and laugh at, so for a bit of light relief, let's take a look at the oddest and most unusual creatures currently walking, flying, or swimming our planet!

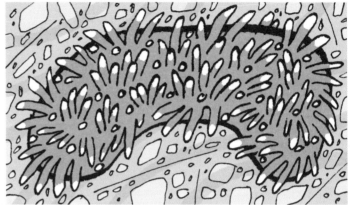

NAKED MOLE RAT

This hairless creature lives underground in East Africa and has four goofy front teeth for tunnelling through sand. "Yuck," you cry. "It eats dirt?!" No – its lips close behind its teeth to keep the dirt out. Mole rats live in groups of

"Mole rats can go for up to half an hour without oxygen and don't feel pain"

up to 300 and all work for a queen – a bit like ants and bees. They're the only mammals to live like this. Only the queen can have babies and she bosses everyone else around. Mole rats can go for up to half an hour without oxygen and don't feel pain – superpowers that make up for looking like an old man with no clothes on. Almost.

POTOO

The potoo is a nocturnal, insect-eating bird from Central and South America. It looks just like a tree branch when it's sitting still, which it does a lot, but it also has a mouth like a cave, eyes like plates and a call like an embarrassed person whistling. If you fancy a pot of potoo for dinner and are planning to sneak up on one when it's asleep, tread carefully – potoos have slits in their eyelids that can sense movement even when their eyes are shut.

SEA CUCUMBERS

Mmm. Cucumber. Fresh, green, cool... but we're talking about the sea creature, not the vegetable. Cool, since it's cold-blooded like all invertebrates, and it cruises the depths of the cold sea floor. Green – yes, though also blue, red, black or brown. Fresh? Yep, and it's eaten by crab, large fish and even human beings (apparently it's slippery and doesn't taste of much). But watch out when you're trying to catch it. The sea cucumber has two weird yet wonderful skills: 1) It can turn itself into liquid and then back into solid form again to escape. 2) It can vomit out its insides along with a revolting acid. Oh yes – and it breathes through its bum. Told you – weird.

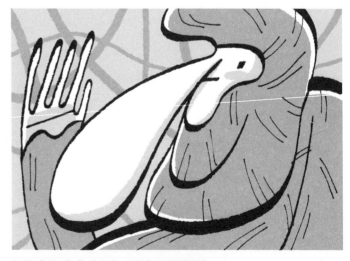

PROBOSCIS MONKEY

Yes, it's got a massive nose. Don't rub it in. If you do, you'll get an earful – its nose acts like a speaker, so its call is really loud. Proboscis monkeys also have slightly webbed feet – they're good swimmers, though they bellyflop into the water from trees, which has got to hurt. They live on the tropical island of Borneo, though, so it's not all bad.

9

SPOT QUIZ!

True OR **False** ?

1. The potoo is a tree from South Africa.

2. Texas horned lizards mostly eat mice.

....

3. Naked mole rats live in a strict hierarchy.

4. Potoos can see with their eyes closed.

....

5. Sea cucumbers can pour themselves through tiny gaps.

6. The proboscis monkey is known for its big arms.

....

10 Create your own weird and wonderful creature and draw it here:

TEXAS HORNED LIZARD
PROFILE

LENGTH: 70–100 mm
WEIGHT: 4.5–5.6 g

 **APPEARANCE:** Like they'd be seriously painful to tread on by mistake – which you might do, because they're so well camouflaged that it's hard to see them.

HABITAT: The prairies and deserts of North America. They're the cowboys of the lizard world.

 **DIET:** Their favourite feast is harvester ants, but when there aren't enough of these around, they chow down any small insect they can find.

CONSERVATION STATUS: Least Concern, which means they're okay, though their numbers are falling. Human pesticides are killing off harvester ant colonies, meaning the lizards can't find enough to eat.

BEHAVIOUR: Pretty chilled. These guys don't have many predators so they spend most of their time basking motionless in the sun.

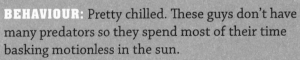 **TOP FACT:** When threatened, Texas horned lizards swell up so they're hard to swallow. They can also shoot a disgusting-tasting stream of blood from their eyes and mouth up to about 1.5 metres. Very offputting.

PRAYING MANTIS
PROFILE

LENGTH: 13 mm–15 cm
WEIGHT: around 170 g

👁 **APPEARANCE:** They're well camouflaged, but if you do see them, they'll be green or brown. They look religious – their forelegs are bent in a way that makes it seem like they're praying.

✥ **HABITAT:** Mantis can be found all over the world, though they mostly live in warm, tropical places, the kind most of us would like to go to on holiday.

🍎 **DIET:** They like their food live and wriggly; they wait, very still, and then grab passing insects. Some species even eat lizards and frogs.

💚 **CONSERVATION STATUS:** NOT endangered – repeat, they are not in danger! Turn up the music and party, mantis!

☯ **BEHAVIOUR:** Sneaky! Much of it consists of keeping verrrry still so predators don't notice them, and so they can surprise insects and gobble them up before the poor things even know what's happening. But we're not judging. We've all got to eat.

❓ **TOP FACT:** Praying mantis also eat each other – and some females actually bite the heads off their boyfriends. Not cool, guys!

DID YOU KNOW?

Check out the amazing differences in the time it takes to grow a baby!

Opossums – 14 days
(Easy peasy)

Elephants – 22 months
(That's almost two years!)

Frilled sharks – 3.5 years
(That's – too long.)

LOVE IS IN THE AIR

Here at *The Zoological Times* we LOVE babies. Especially the edible ones. (Just joking!) But we think it's time we celebrated all the parents out there, too. After all, none of us would exist without them! Every month, we'll bring you some of the best love stories from the animal kingdom.

Swans are a wonderful example of long-lasting love. Quite often, a swan will find true love when they are only two years old and stay with their partner, raising many cygnets (that's swan babies to you and me), until death does them part – and let's not forget, some swans can live for thirty years! Female swans usually lay 3–8 eggs at a time, so that's a lot of babies. How DO they do it? We ask Sid and Cecily, a lovely couple of mute swans from Brockwell Park, London, about their lives together.

So Sid - what's your secret?
Sid: Eh? How do you know about that? It was years ago and Terry promised he wouldn't tell anyone!

Er, no sorry, your secret to a long and happy relationship...?
Sid: Oh, that.
Cecily: Take no notice of him. He's just busking.

Busking? Ah! Here's 20p.

Cecily: No, that's what it's called when we swans get cross. Some say we're strong enough to break the arm of a human, but we're not that aggressive really. When we snap and flap, it's usually to protect our young.

Your young! Yes, let's talk more about that.

Cecily: Well, we lay around seven eggs a year, in the spring or early summer, and then we take turns to sit on them, don't we love?

Sid: We do. Takes about five or six weeks for them to hatch, doesn't it?

Cecily: Indeed it does. Sid and I share all the responsibilities. He finds the stuff for the nest and I build it; I lay the eggs, obviously, but he's usually the one to sit on them and incubate them so I can feed myself up again. It takes a lot out of you, egg-laying.

Sid: Yeah, and we watch out for each other, too. We're a good team when it comes to seeing off threats and making sure the little 'uns are alright.

Cecily: Mmm – and when our little cygnets hatch, we have a lovely time looking after them and teaching them things.

Sid, misty-eyed: Sometimes I give 'em rides on my back.

Aww – how lovely.

Cecily: Yes it is. Then, when they're about six months or so, we chase 'em away.

Sid: Yep. We just turn on them, out of nowhere. Bye bye babies – time to go and find your own flock.

I... I see. But you don't chase each other away, do you?

Sid: Oh no, we're ever so close.

Cecily: Ooh no, we wouldn't do that.

So, what's the best thing about being in a long relationship like yours?

Cecily: Well, I think what's lovely is that we've been through so much together, and we've learned from our past mistakes, particularly when it comes to bringing up babies. We just get better and better at it.

Sid: Especially at chasing them away.

Cecily: Yes.

And with that, the happy couple smile and look lovingly into each other's eyes. Well! If that's not romance, I don't know what is.

Look out for more classic love stories from animals that mate for life: albatross, barn owls, beavers and wolves!

❝ ODD ONE OUT

Bowerbirds, which live in the forests of New Guinea and Australia, have a heart-melting way of finding a partner. They build an elaborate arch out of leaves and twigs, then decorate it with all the most colourful things they can find, including berries and fruit, petals, shiny pieces of metal and brightly coloured plastic. Adorable! Which of the following items CAN'T you find in this close-up of a bower bird's courtship arch?

STRAW

RING PULL

DEFLATED BALLOON

KEY

SAFETY PIN

PENCIL

FEATHER

TOY CAR

COIN

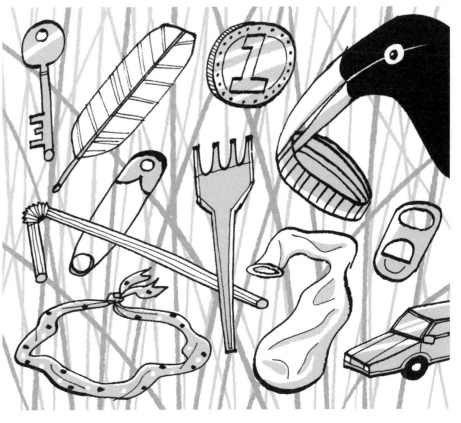

FOOD & DRINK

WHO NEEDS TABLE MANNERS?

Not us! There are all sorts of ways to enjoy your food and drink, and they're all fine by us. As long as we aren't the ones being eaten.

DRINKING

Butterflies don't have mouths, so they can't bite or chew their food – they drink it. When a butterfly lands on a flower, it tastes the sweetness of the pollen through its feet (hope it washes them first). Then it unfurls the long, curled straw attached to its head (called a "proboscis") and drinks up the nectar. Handy! Spiders don't have teeth to chew with, though they do have fangs to inject venom into their victims with – ouch! The venom kills their prey and turns its insides into mush, which the spider then sucks up. Delicious.

LICK TRICKS

Anteaters have no teeth for chewing, either, just a massively long tongue covered in loads of tiny hooks and sticky spit. Moving this really fast from side to side the anteater can gather hundreds of insects in one sweep. All the gross dirt it licks up at the same time helps it crush and digest its lunch.

REGURGITATING

Food coming back up is yuck, right? Not for "ruminants" like antelopes, deer, sheep and cattle. Regurgitating food keeps them safe! How? Well, out in the open, where they may be spotted by a predator, they eat as much vegetation as they can, as quickly as possible. Then they go somewhere safe to digest it. Cunning! Ruminants' stomachs have compartments, so when they've found their safe place, their "storage stomach" sends food back up for them to chew on slowly and swallow again. Yum.

"Ruminants' stomachs have compartments. Their 'storage stomach' sends food back up for them to chew on slowly and swallow again. Yum"

SWALLOWING ALIVE

Then there are those who just open wide and swallow their food whole, leaving their stomachs to do the hard work. Pelicans do this with fish, owls do it with small rodents, and some snakes do it with creatures much, much bigger than they are – their skin just sort of stretches around their prey. Cool! (Though it can make them look a bit weird.)

⑫ SCAVENGER HUNT

Valerie Vulture has spotted a delicious dead antelope. It's decaying pretty fast though! Help her find her way through the maze to her dinner.

BOA CONSTRICTOR
PROFILE

LENGTH: 4 m
WEIGHT: 27 kg

APPEARANCE: Long, wiggly and covered in red, yellow or green patterns, depending on where they live – they like to blend into the background. Don't look at the pretty patterns for too long though or... oops!

HABITAT: These guys like it warm and humid; they hang out in Central and South America, living in hollow tree trunks or old burrows in the ground.

DIET: You! Seriously, they chow down pretty much anything, from rodents to ocelots (a kind of leopard) and wild pigs. They just open wide and swallow you whole!

CONSERVATION STATUS: Some species are endangered – humans hunt them for their skin.

BEHAVIOUR: They're top ambushers. A boa constrictor can tell if something yummy is hurrying past by flicking out its tongue – it can taste its prey in the air. Then it POUNCES, sinking its teeth into the poor creature before wrapping itself around it and slowly squeeeeezing until its prey is dead.

TOP FACT: Momma boas can have up to 60 two-foot-long babies at a time!

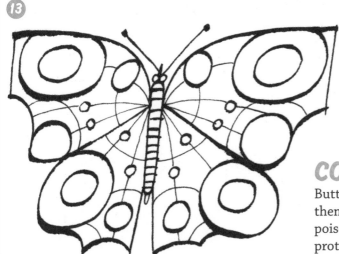

13

COULD A FREEGAN LIFESTYLE BE FOR YOU?

We all know that food can be costly – as a hunter, you can even end up paying for it with your life, either through injury or starving to death when there isn't enough to catch.

But freegans such as the Egyptian vulture have found an ingenious way to make sure there's lots of free food wherever they go: they eat... poo! (Amongst other things). We spoke to Edna and Vera, two Egyptian vultures from Spain (they admit their name is misleading; these birds can be found across much of the world). They told us about their "freegan" lifestyle. "Being a freegan means we don't believe in wasting," explains Edna. "So we clean up for other animals, eating their leftovers and whatnot. We do it for selfless reasons.

> *"Being a freegan means we don't believe in wasting things."*

If we eat what other animals leave behind, then there's more of the fresh stuff for everyone else!"

I point out that scavenging like this isn't entirely selfless – it's easier than hunting fresh meat, which has a habit of running away. "Well yes," agrees Edna, reluctantly. "But we do see it as a public service."

"Yeah," interrupts Vera. "Also, poo is full of this stuff called carotenoid which makes our faces yellow. And a yellow face

The griffon vulture: another well-known freegan. It prefers dead animals to poo, though

tells other vultures, 'I'm so healthy, I can even eat poo and survive!' Which is great for attracting a mate."

Whatever the reasons behind their freeganism, there's no doubt that it provides the Egyptian vulture with a cheap and easy way of getting food. It's a great idea, so long as you're not too fussy about what you eat.

COLOURING IN SAVES LIVES

Butterflies' wings aren't just for show – the bright colours help them blend into the background or warn predators that they're poisonous and dangerous to eat! Colour this butterfly in and protect it from being munched.

A lick a day keeps the doctor away

WOUND LICKING: THE BENEFITS

We've all been there – a quick snarl at a stranger and, before you know it, they've lashed out and you've got a nasty scratch. It's bleeding; it's stinging. If you don't do something fast, it's going to get infected.

Many of us know which plants to nibble when we're sick, thanks to the wisdom our parents have passed on. The chimpanzees of Tanzania know to eat the bitter leaves of the vernonia plant when they have an upset tummy, and South American parrots eat dirt (literally) to absorb harmful poisons from the seeds they love munching on. But how do you stop a scratch from going bad? Well, it's simple – just lick it! You may find you do this instinctively – even human beings do. Spit cleans the wound and has antiseptic qualities, meaning it kills harmful bacteria. So next time you're on the wrong end of a sharp claw, lick for your life!

⑭ COMPETITION CORNER:

What's the most beautiful creature you can imagine? Draw it here.

ELEPHANT PROFILE

HEIGHT: 2.7–3.3 m
WEIGHT: 2,700–6,000 kg

APPEARANCE: Otherworldly, like great, wrinkly aliens. There are only two kinds of elephant left: African and Asian. You can tell them apart by their ears – Asian elephants have smaller ears, and African elephants would get teased for their giant flappers if they couldn't just stand on you to shut you up.

HABITAT: The African elephant lives in Africa and the Asian elephant lives in Asia, so that's nice and easy to remember. Asian elephants like hot forests and African elephants live anywhere there is food and water: rainforests, savannahs and even desert.

DIET: Leaves, grass, small bushes – tasty veggies.

CONSERVATION STATUS: Asian elephants are endangered and African elephants are vulnerable, which means they'll probably be endangered soon.

BEHAVIOUR: Females live together in herds and males usually live on their own. They laugh, cry, grieve for their dead and have incredibly long memories. They are generally some of the nicest and most intelligent creatures you'll come across.

TOP FACT: These guys are the only mammals that can't jump.

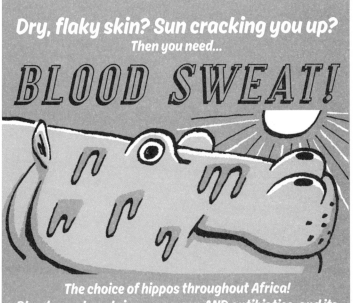
15 Can you find the five words listed below amongst this muddle? They could go in any direction – even backwards!

CLAW, MACAW, SEEDS, WOUND, MANE

C	G	E	P	F	H	S	N
L	Q	G	S	H	K	E	W
A	A	B	R	S	C	E	O
W	M	A	C	A	W	D	U
X	A	L	T	E	N	S	N
H	E	U	T	G	P	G	D
Y	L	D	E	N	A	M	L

BE THE MANE MAN!

Big, shaggy manes: they're to die for!

A good mane roars, "I'm strong, I'm powerful: don't mess". Manes get darker with age, warning any little squirts looking for a fight that you're experienced and you know how to fight. A scraggy mane, on the other hand, is an embarrassment. It tells the world you can't catch enough food and that you've probably come off worse in a few punch-ups. So mane-taining is important.

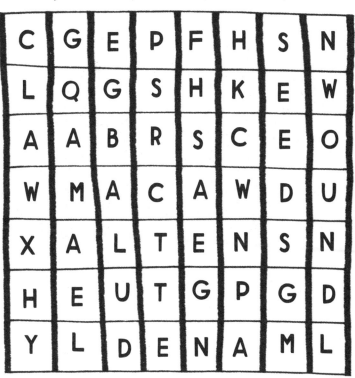

Lions who live in warmer climates have thinner manes as their bodies shed hair to keep cool, so as the world heats up it's getting more important to care for your hair.

HERE ARE SOME TIPS:

EAT WELL –
A rich diet with plenty of meat will keep your mane thick and glossy.

BAN BUGS –
Ticks and other nuisance insects can live in your mane, sucking your blood and suchlike. Get your cubs to have a good scratch about to get 'em out!

SHADY CHARACTER –
Stay in the shade whenever you can. The hot sun plus a thick mane is enough to boil anyone's brains – plus the heat might actually make your mane thinner!

A magnificent mane.
Picture taken: in a hurry

I WILL SURVIVE

Let's face it: in the animal kingdom, staying healthy pretty much just means staying alive.

In the wild, we have to deal with starvation, water shortages and predators. We can't do much if there's not enough to eat and drink, but we CAN get tips on how to avoid being eaten. Let's take a look at how some of the pros do it!

CAMOUFLAGE

Disguising yourself so you blend into the background is the best way to keep safe from predators – plus it means your own prey won't spot you when you're hunting them! Camouflage works for creatures great and small, from leopards with spots that make them blend in with the forest shade to insects that look exactly like twigs. Some animals don't have permanent markings – chameleons change colour to match their environment and the incredible mimic octopus can alter its appearance to look like at least fifteen other completely different species!

BLUFFING

Also known as the handicap principle, there's a clever kind of mind game that's pretty much the opposite of camouflage. When you're being chased by a predator, try saying, "Over here, sucker! I'm not scared of you – you'll never catch me!" It might just put them off or confuse them – they're used to creatures bolting in terror at the mere sight of them. It's pretty risky, but hey, it's worth a shot when you have nothing to lose! Gazelles do little skippety jumps when they see a lion or cheetah, as if to say, "Come on, you fat old loser – I'd like to see you try." The predator might decide not to waste energy chasing such a fit young gazelle and look for an older, slower model instead. Larks sing when being hunted by merlin falcons, as if to say, "This is so easy – I'm not even trying." This discourages the falcons and they sometimes just give up the chase!

SPEED

Another top tip for self defence is simply to run away! The cheetah is the undisputed king of the race, sometimes sprinting at speeds of around 100 km/h. But cheetahs can only do this for short distances, while gazelles – their favourite food – can run nearly as fast and keep up their speed for far longer, giving them a chance of getting away. The ostrich is commonly thought to bury its head in the sand when danger approaches, but this isn't true – at a sniff of danger, ostriches leg it, at super speeds of 70 km/h!

ARMOUR

Some might say this is the best form of defence. Most predators leave hippos and elephants alone, not only because of their sheer size, but also because chewing through their five-centimetre-thick hide is more trouble than it's worth. A prickly hide like a giant dragon lizard's is not top of the menu for most predators, either. No one wants a mouthful of spikes for their supper.

⑯ FUNKY SKUNK

Copy the drawing below, using the squares to guide you.

AXOLOTL PROFILE

LENGTH: 23 cm
WEIGHT: 120–180 g

👁 **APPEARANCE:** From the front, it looks like a cute, rubbery toy with delicate little hands. From the side, it looks like a fishy lizard.

✛ **HABITAT:** Axolotl are amphibious – they can live on land as well as in water. They have only ever been found in two lakes in Mexico. One lake no longer exists, and the other has been turned into a series of canals, which is a bit like someone building a carpark in your living room.

🍎 **DIET:** Small worms, fish and insects. Axolotl have no teeth, so they have to suck their food up as it passes, like an old man without his dentures.

♥ **CONSERVATION STATUS:** Possibly extinct in the wild – waah! Lots of people keep them as pets though, so they still exist.

☯ **BEHAVIOUR:** A bit of swimming, a bit of walking, a bit of eating fish.

❓ **TOP FACT:** Okay – this is amazing. Axolotls can heal themselves. Like magic! They can grow new limbs and even replace damaged parts of their own brain. They're the superheroes of the natural world.

⑰ COMPETITION CORNER:

Sometimes there's nothing for it – you just have to stand your ground and fight. Can you match each of these defence mechanisms to the right creature?

| INK | QUILLS | HORN | SMELL | BLOOD SPURTS |

| RHINO | OCTOPUS | PORCUPINE | TEXAS HORNED LIZARD | SKUNK |

FOCUS ON: LANGURS

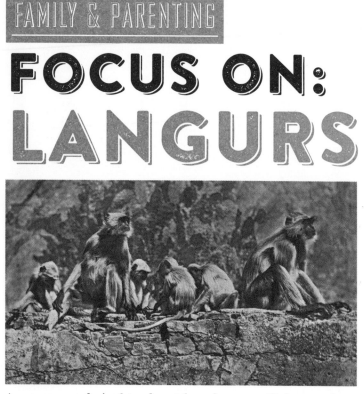

As anyone who's friends with a langur will know, these monkeys put family first – at least the female ones do. I can't count the number of times my BFF, Lucy Langur, has cancelled on me so she can hang out with her sisters, mother and aunties. Langur ladies like nothing better than playing with each other, picking fleas out of each other's hair and generally chillaxing. They look after each other's kids and everyone helps out foraging for food. Langur males, on the other hand, are a bit more fighty and like to be in charge. Often there's just one in a group with lots of females, but if there's more than one, the boys will fight to show who's boss. Sometimes a whole group of males will go off and be fighty on their own for a bit. Probably for the best.

CAMEL PROFILE

HEIGHT: 1.7–2 m
WEIGHT: 400–1000 kg

👁 **APPEARANCE:** A bit like a horse with bad teeth and a hunchback (if it's a dromedary camel, or two hunchbacks if it's a Bactrian).

✛ **HABITAT:** These guys like wide open spaces, like deserts or plains.

🍎 **DIET:** Strictly veggie.

♥ **CONSERVATION STATUS:** Wild dromedary camels are extinct, but there are lots of domesticated ones and feral ones (descended from escaped domesticated camels). There are plenty of domesticated Bactrians as well, but only about 1,000 in the wild.

BEHAVIOUR: Camels blow on each other's faces to say hi. They can run for long distances and store fat and moisture in their humps to live off when supplies are scarce. If they spit on you (it's actually vomit), it's because they feel threatened. So, you know, it's understandable.

❓ **TOP FACT:** Camels can live for up to SIX MONTHS without food or water!

18 WHAT COMES NEXT?

Look at these patterns and work out what's next in the sequence.

MONKEY PANDA ? PANDA MONKEY PANDA

BIRD BIRD MONKEY BIRD BIRD MONKEY BIRD ? MONKEY

HUMAN ? BIRD HUMAN MONKEY BIRD

ASK CLARE

Let our resident crane supernanny answer your problems!

DEAR CLARE,

My friends say I let my children (literally) walk all over me. I suppose I do, but I love them so much I feel like I could die for them – again, literally. After I've laid my eggs, I watch over them until they hatch, eating as much as I can lay my fangs on to stock up on really good nutrients. I also break down most of my own insides into healthy juices to feed them, which can be a bit ouchy. By the time my gorgeous bubbas hatch, I'm a walking husk of my former self! I regurgitate all this good stuff into their hungry little mouths – I know!! What am I like?! – and once I've fed them, I let them crawl on to me and sink their venom into me so what's left of my insides turns to mush. Then they eat me alive, bless them! Do you think I spoil them?

Yours respectfully, Donna Desert Spider

Clare says…
Dear Donna, You live – and die – for your children, and I can't think of a nobler cause. But try to do something just for you once in a while. Why not squeeze in a jog every so often, or treat yourself to a massage while your babies are sucking up your liquefied insides? The happier you are, the happier those little cuties will be! *Love Clare*

DEAR CLARE,

I can't shake the feeling that there's something not quite right about one of my hatchlings. It came out of an egg that looked slightly different from all the rest, but I didn't think anything of it at the time. But when it hatched, it shoved all the other eggs and hatchlings out of the nest. It's also massive – about three times the size of my usual chicks – and it wants feeding constantly. I'm exhausted! Then, the other day, I could have sworn I heard it go "cuckoo!". What's wrong with it?

Please help, Rebecca Reed Warbler

Clare says…
Dear Rebecca, You've been well and truly tricked, my dear. It sounds as though you turned your back on your nest for a moment and a cheeky cuckoo flew down, tipped one of your eggs out of your nest and laid her own. It only takes a minute, girl, and it happens all the time. The hatchling you're half killing yourself to bring up is 100% cuckoo. My advice? Be more careful next time! *Love Clare*

DEAR CLARE,

Humans think I'm really cute and cuddly – they like pandas so much that they've put us on special protection lists – but I have a problem that I think will make me less popular. The thing is, when I have twins I have to make sure that the strongest one survives, even if it means the other one dies. It's an awful decision to have to make, but if there isn't enough food to go around, it's better to end up with one well-fed, strong cub than two hungry weak ones, especially when there are so few of us around. I have to go for the best chance of survival. Am I a bad panda? Will humans hate me?

Yours, Polly Panda

Clare says…
Dear Polly, No you are NOT a bad panda! You're not the only creature that has to make this difficult choice – many species do. Earwigs can have 60 babies ("nymphs") and know more than half will die, so they concentrate on looking after the healthy ones. It's sad, but it's a fact. Humans won't take you off the endangered list – they feel too guilty because they've destroyed half of your natural habitat. Thanks for sharing, Polly. *Love, Clare*

⑲ WHERE ARE YOU, WARBLER?
Can you help this reed warbler find her way back to her nest?

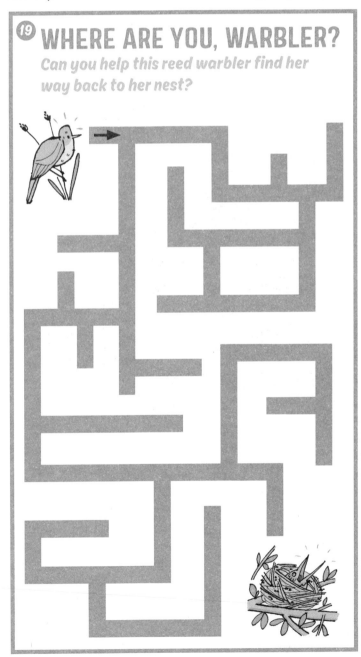

ENVIRONMENT

BACK IN THE HABITAT

Some animals like the wide-open spaces of the African grasslands. Some prefer the rainforest, where food literally grows on trees (if you like eating leaves – and who doesn't?).

Others live in the creepiest depths of the ocean, where the pressure is so great it could crush your bones. But we're not judging! (Although – have you seen an angler fish recently?) Luckily, however strange your tastes, there's a habitat to suit you somewhere on Earth.

Mountains offer great selfie opportunities for brown bears

RAINFOREST

Like trees? Want to feel damp and sweaty pretty much all the time? The rainforest is for you! Located at the equator, the imaginary line around the middle of the world, the rainforest is rainy, green and full of life. Tall trees form canopies over the forest, so you won't get much sunlight at ground level. Howler monkeys howl, puffins pluck fruit with their colourful beaks, giant blue morpho butterflies flit through the air and sloths sort of just hang around all the time, hoping that no one will notice them.

WOODLAND

Fond of trees, not that keen on the heat? Welcome to the woodland. Whether you're high up near mountains or low down near a river, trees provide shelter for deer, squirrels and rabbits, and there are plenty of nuts, fruit and insects to go around. Hear hammering? That could be a woodpecker, drilling into tree bark to find grubs to eat. Hear hooting? That might be an owl, chatting with its chicks. Hear a terrifying growl? That's probably an angry brown bear. Run!

GRASSLAND

Maybe you don't like trees. Maybe you prefer a nice uninterrupted view of the sky. Maybe all you want is a bit of peace and quiet, grass to eat, and somewhere flat to run around. Is that too much to ask? No! Grassland provides all this and more, whether you're a zebra grazing in the African savannah or an anteater hanging out in the Llanos of South America. Just watch out for lions and jaguars. And fires.

FRESHWATER

There's nothing nicer than a fast-flowing river, or a lovely stagnant pond, particularly if you're a fish, or a worm, or some sort of amphibian, or an insect... All sorts of creatures live in freshwater, eating the vegetation or each other. So it's a shame that humans keep polluting rivers and streams, and that ponds have gone out of fashion.

OCEAN

If you like variety, the ocean is the place for you. As long as you can breathe underwater. From the warm waters around coral reefs to murky deep-ocean trenches and the freezing ice caps of the North Pole, there's something for everyone. You'll find whales, turtles, creatures like coral that look like they belong in a garden centre, and lots and lots of fish – including the angler fish, a deep-sea fish with a luminous fishing-rod thing to lure creatures into its nasty jaws. Like I say: creepy.

The angler fish: best avoided

DESERT

If you don't like carrying an umbrella and don't get thirsty much, try the desert. You have to be able to withstand scorching heat and find cunning ways to conserve water and food – there isn't much around – so having a fat-filled hump is a bonus (shout out to all the camels out there). It's best to hide all day and search for food at night, so hopefully you have good night vision. But be warned: the desert can be deadly boring. And pretty deadly in general.

TRAVEL REPORT:
HAROLD HIPPOPOTAMUS TAKES A SPA BREAK IN THE RIVERS OF SUB-SAHARAN AFRICA

After a long week attacking local crocodiles, stealing crops from farmers and fighting other males to the death, there's nothing like retreating to shallow water for a bit of me-time. Here in the rivers and lakes of southern Africa, you can kick back and relax for up to sixteen hours a day. I'm lucky, me – I secrete my own natural sun cream, so there's no risk of getting burned! At sunset, my friends and I leave the water and head inland for dinner. We usually opt for the fresh local grass – so moreish! Then it's back to the river for an underwater snooze. Five stars.

POLAR BEAR
PROFILE

LENGTH: 2–3 m
WEIGHT: 150–450 kg

APPEARANCE: Like large, white teddy bears with huge claws (ie don't try to cuddle them). They're the world's biggest land carnivores (though they mostly live in the sea and on ice. But let's not be pedantic).

HABITAT: The Arctic Ocean, at the North Pole.

DIET: Polar bears eat seals, and can sniff them out from over a kilometre away. A bear waits on sea ice till a seal comes up for air, and then BAM! The seal's dead. That's nature for you.

CONSERVATION STATUS: Vulnerable. Climate change means sea ice in the North Pole is melting, making it harder for polar bears to find food.

BEHAVIOUR: Polar bears spend most of their time alone, but sometimes they like to playfight. And why not? There's not much else to do in the Arctic. They're not aggressive when they're well fed, but if they're hungry, watch out – they get a bit bitey.

TOP FACT: Polar bears have black skin, but their see-through fur reflects light, so they look white.

⑳ WHO LIVES IN A HABITAT LIKE THIS?

See if you can match the animal to their home.

SLOTH

GRASSLAND

OWL

OCEAN

ZEBRA

WOOD

TURTLE

RAINFOREST

CHEETAH!

The Animal Olympics took place last week, and once again, the games were marred by controversy.

A lion representing Kenya was disqualified from the 200-metre race when traces of catnip were found in her system. And the 100-metre sprint turned out to be the end of the road for one poor pronghorn antelope. Our reporter, Wilma Weasel, has the details.

100-METRE SPRINT TURNS DEADLY

Chester Cheetah won the 100-metre sprint in an amazing 5.95 seconds. The crowds cheered – but the mood turned sour when Chester, not content with being the fastest land animal on the planet, proceeded to eat Pernilla Pronghorn Antelope, who came in second. "He's always been competitive," said Brian Blue Wildebeest, who placed third. "He knew that pronghorn antelopes are the fastest animals on Earth over long distances, and he wanted to get Pernilla out of the way before the

1,500 metres." But Chester's plan backfired. Judges stripped him of his medal and awarded Pernilla the gold medal posthumously. Luella Lion, who came in fourth, said she couldn't be happier with her unexpected bronze medal. "I never stand a chance when there's a cheetah in the race," she told us.

KANGAROO CONFUSION

Karly Kangaroo missed out on a place in the 100-metre sprint, as she had to comfort her daughter, Kelly, who was extremely upset after losing her under-fives' bouncing race. Later, she told our reporter she was thanking her lucky stars not to have made it back to the starting line in time. "I had a lucky escape," she said. "That Chester is a liability. There's a reason we don't have cheetahs in Australia."

21 SPOT THE DIFFERENCE

Twins Terry and Terri Tiger went head to head in the wrestling final. Surprise surprise – it was a draw! See if you can spot six differences between these pictures of them in action.

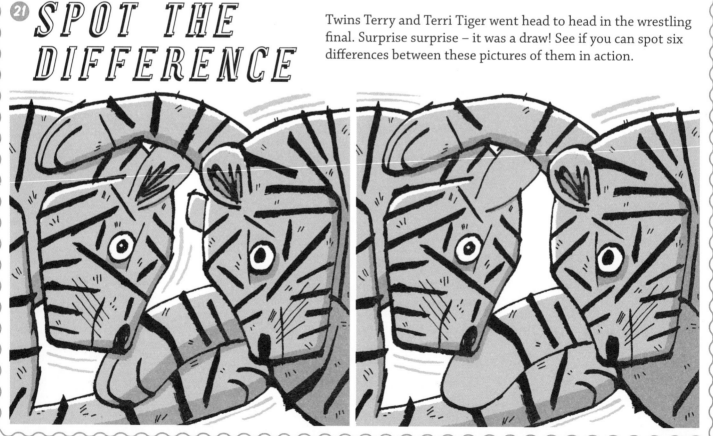

SWIM IF YOU'RE WINNING

It was pointy nose v. pointy nose in the front crawl final. Marvin Black Marlin narrowly beat Enya Sail Fish, swimming at an incredible 130 kilometres per hour to hold on to his world record. Further down the scoreboard, there was no "Wahoo!" from Wendy Wahoo – she came in a disappointing fourth place, narrowly defeated by Marvin's cousin, Marlon Striped Marlin. "He may have the gold medal, but I have the looks," Marlon said, showing off his delightful striped scales.

SMALL BUT MIGHTY

Griselda Gorilla was a little put out, to say the least, when she lost out on the weight-lifting medal to three creatures a fraction of her size. "Look, right," she said, "I lifted 2,500 kg. That's the weight of 30 humans. That's WAY more than those runty little creatures managed!" Griselda has a point – but, as the judges pointed out, 2,500 kg is only ten times Griselda's bodyweight. Drew Dung Beetle pulled a small lump of poo across the ground to claim the gold medal – but that

poo was 1,141 times his own weight. Reggie Rhinoceros Beetle lifted a lump of wood 850 times his weight and Lesley Leafcutter Ant, who won bronze, bench-pressed a leaf 50 times her weight. Sorry, Griselda – but at least you're not having dung for dinner! Bon appetit, Drew.

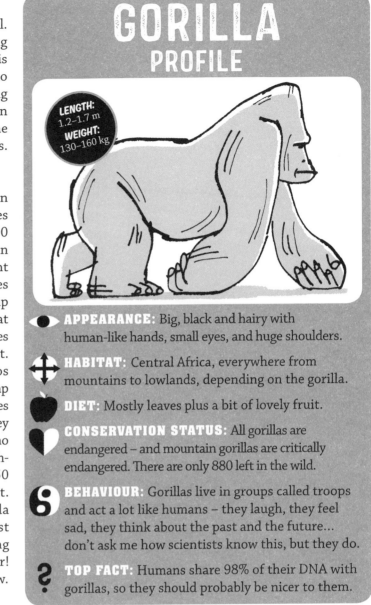

GORILLA
PROFILE

LENGTH: 1.2–1.7 m
WEIGHT: 130–160 kg

- **APPEARANCE:** Big, black and hairy with human-like hands, small eyes, and huge shoulders.

- **HABITAT:** Central Africa, everywhere from mountains to lowlands, depending on the gorilla.

- **DIET:** Mostly leaves plus a bit of lovely fruit.

- **CONSERVATION STATUS:** All gorillas are endangered – and mountain gorillas are critically endangered. There are only 880 left in the wild.

- **BEHAVIOUR:** Gorillas live in groups called troops and act a lot like humans – they laugh, they feel sad, they think about the past and the future… don't ask me how scientists know this, but they do.

- **TOP FACT:** Humans share 98% of their DNA with gorillas, so they should probably be nicer to them.

22 DOT-TO-DOT

Join the dots to find out who won the synchronized swimming contest.

SIXTH SENSE

Spectators flocked in their thousands to watch the Great Sense Challenge this weekend, in which animals from around the globe used their weird and wonderful bodies to figure out what was going on around them.

"This event is a celebration of the amazing range of abilities we have in the animal kingdom, from fantastic hearing to brilliant eyesight to other more... niche skills, shall we say," said Eli Elephant, Head of the Animal Committee. As ever, there was controversy about how such different skills can be compared. "You can't really say that one ability is better than another," agrees Eli. "The judges are looking at how well each creature performs its own speciality." Here's a quick look at how some of the competitors fared.

NAME:
Barry

SPECIES:
Black Widow Spider

CATEGORY:
Vibration detection

PERFORMANCE:
Barry's challenge was to approach two females – Brenda and Belinda – and suss out which was less likely to eat him. Barry has poor vision, like most spiders, despite being endowed with eight eyes. He doesn't have a nose or ears, so he can't hear or smell, either. But the fine hairs on his eight magnificent legs detect the slightest movement – even sound waves in the air – and translate them into noise. The hairs can also detect scent from females and "read" information such as how recently they have eaten... and how hungry they are.

JUDGE'S VERDICT: Sadly, Barry's legs let him down. He thought Brenda was the safest female – wrong! There's a reason these spiders are named "widows". RIP Barry. 0/10

NAME:
Denny

SPECIES:
Bottlenose Dolphin

CATEGORY:
Echolocation

PERFORMANCE:
Denny found his way through the sea using echolocation. This involves producing a series of clicks to send sound waves through the water. When these waves encounter an object, they bounce off and travel back to Denny, who can feel them in his forehead and work out what the object is, where it's heading and how fast it's travelling.

JUDGE'S VERDICT: Denny made his way elegantly through the water, despite only being able to see about half a metre ahead of him. He correctly identified that, from the tone and speed of the echoes, there was a shark heading straight for him, at which point he flipped fin and shot off in the opposite direction before he could claim his prize. Well done Denny! 10/10

NAME:
Alan

SPECIES:
Arctic Tern

CATEGORY:
Sense of Direction

PERFORMANCE:
Alan set off from the Arctic in September and arrived, sooner even than he was expected, last Friday at teatime. Arctic terns are known for the extraordinary distances they cover each year; they use landmarks such as the stars and distinctive coastlines to find their way as they criss-cross the world from pole to pole, chasing summer from one end of the Earth to the other. They're also able to sense the Earth's magnetic field with a sort of chemical compass in their bodies. Amazing! These long-haul fliers can cover around 2.4 million km in their lifetime, That's like flying to the moon and back more than three times!

> *"That's like flying to the moon and back more than three times!"*

JUDGE'S VERDICT: Alan travelled over 93,000 km, only stopping for a few breaks. This bird is going places – quite literally! 11/10

NAME:
Colin

SPECIES:
Cockroach

CATEGORY:
Seeing in the dark

PERFORMANCE:
Colin beat Nancy, an Indian nocturnal carpenter bee in the qualifiers, to become this year's Seeing-in-the-Dark Champion, though it was a very close-run thing. "I can see in almost pitch black," explains Colin, proudly. "Pretty useful when I'm scuttling about under cupboards looking for grub!"

JUDGE'S VERDICT: Colin was up against some impressive competition this year – cats and tarsiers were both high on our selection list, and both species are distinctly cuter than cockroaches. But in the end we put our prejudices aside, because Colin's night vision beats the rest hands down. 9/10 (Point off for not being cute.)

W	G	E	P	H	I	S	O	U	N	D	T	B
I	T	B	I	F	L	T	G	S	H	K	M	F
D	A	S	P	I	D	E	R	U	T	S	E	R
O	L	O	C	H	Y	R	E	T	O	E	A	O
W	N	U	E	N	C	N	L	D	O	N	G	A
B	P	N	X	V	I	Y	R	A	L	S	T	C
G	M	D	O	L	P	H	I	N	B	E	A	H
C	O	C	K	R	O	A	C	H	S	T	L	G

23 **Can you find the eight words listed below amongst this muddle?**

SPIDER, TERN, DOLPHIN, SOUND, ROACH, SENSE, WIDOW, COCKROACH

24 *SPOT QUIZ!*

Were you concentrating when you read the Sixth Sense article? Cover it up and test yourself in this true or false quiz.

1. Arctic terns fly around the world so they can follow the cold weather.

2. Cats have good night vision.

....

3. Spiders can see really well with their eight eyes.

4. Female black widow spiders eat males.

....

5. Cockroaches can't see in the dark.

6. Dolphins use their sense of smell to find their way through water.

....

TARANTULA
PROFILE

LENGTH: 11–28 cm
WEIGHT: 28–85 g

APPEARANCE: Like a cuddly, snuggly kitten. With eight legs. And eight eyes. Oh, and fangs.

HABITAT: Scared of tarantulas? Then don't go to South or Central America or Africa. Tarantulas mostly live in burrows. They sometimes weave silken doors or trip wires to detect prey. Tree-dwelling tarantulas live in tunnel-like webs.

DIET: Depends on their size (there are over 700 species of tarantula) – insects, frogs and mice or birds. They pounce on their prey, injecting venom with their fangs that turns their victim's insides to mush, and then suck it up like a meaty smoothie.

CONSERVATION STATUS: Not too bad, though the destruction of the rainforest affects some species.

BEHAVIOUR: Like most of us – they hunt, eat, sleep and make the occasional toilet trip.

TOP FACT: Tarantulas shoot spiky hairs from their legs at predators. The hairs contain enough venom to kill a small mammal. Pa-zoing!

COMPETITION ANSWERS

How did you do in the puzzles? Have you sent your answers to us via pigeon post? If so, check them here! If you haven't, no cheating! We're looking at you, Chester Cheetah... actually, we're running away from you, quite fast.

1
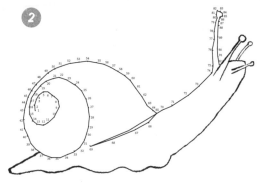

2

3

4
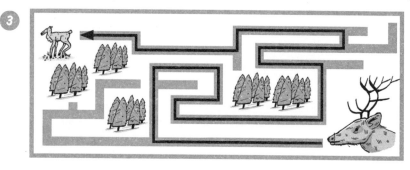

5

VAMPIRE BAT	VAMPIRE BAT	TIGER	VAMPIRE BAT	VAMPIRE BAT	TIGER
TIGER	GOAT	TIGER	GOAT	TIGER	GOAT
VAMPIRE BAT	GOAT	TIGER	VAMPIRE BAT	GOAT	TIGER

6

FLASH QUIZ!

1. A male tiger and female lion produce a liger.

FALSE – A LIGER IS THE BABY OF A MALE LION AND A FEMALE TIGER

2. The Earth's magnetic pull runs from East to West.

FALSE – IT RUNS FROM NORTH TO SOUTH

3. Vampire bats don't really feed on blood, despite their name.

FALSE

4. Okapis aren't very sociable animals.

TRUE

5. Ibex goats can jump to heights of over three metres.

TRUE

6. Vampire bats live alone.

FALSE – THEY LIVE IN GROUPS

7

GINRASH SI
SHARING IS
RAGNIC
CARING

8

9

SPOT QUIZ!

1. The potoo is a tree from South Africa.

FALSE – IT'S A BIRD

2. Texas horned lizards mostly eat mice.

FALSE – THEY EAT ANTS

3. Naked mole rats live in a strict hierarchy.

TRUE

4. Potoos can see with their eyes closed.

TRUE

5. Sea cucumbers can pour themselves through tiny gaps.

TRUE

6. The proboscis monkey is known for its long arms.

FALSE – IT'S KNOWN FOR ITS BIG NOSE

11

THE PENCIL IS THE ODD ONE OUT

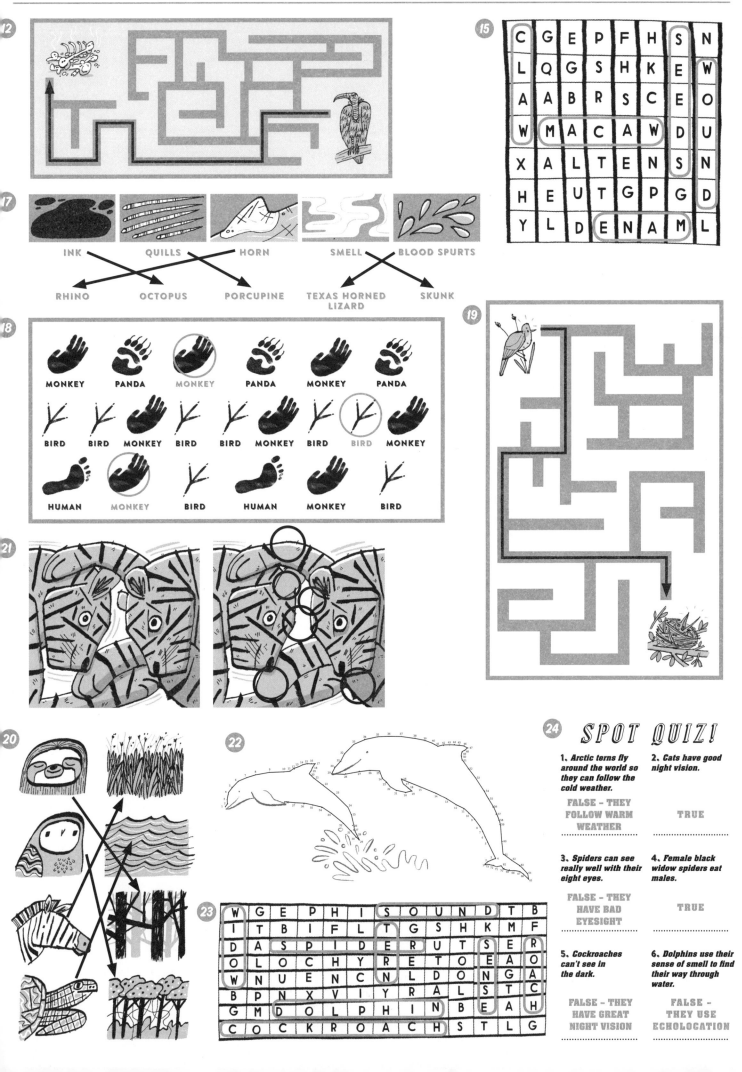

17.
INK · QUILLS · HORN · SMELL · BLOOD SPURTS
RHINO · OCTOPUS · PORCUPINE · TEXAS HORNED LIZARD · SKUNK

18.
MONKEY · PANDA · MONKEY · PANDA · MONKEY · PANDA
BIRD · BIRD · MONKEY · BIRD · BIRD · MONKEY · BIRD · MONKEY
HUMAN · MONKEY · BIRD · HUMAN · MONKEY · BIRD

24. SPOT QUIZ!

1. Arctic terns fly around the world so they can follow the cold weather.

FALSE – THEY FOLLOW WARM WEATHER

2. Cats have good night vision.

TRUE

3. Spiders can see really well with their eight eyes.

FALSE – THEY HAVE BAD EYESIGHT

4. Female black widow spiders eat males.

TRUE

5. Cockroaches can't see in the dark.

FALSE – THEY HAVE GREAT NIGHT VISION

6. Dolphins use their sense of smell to find their way through water.

FALSE – THEY USE ECHOLOCATION

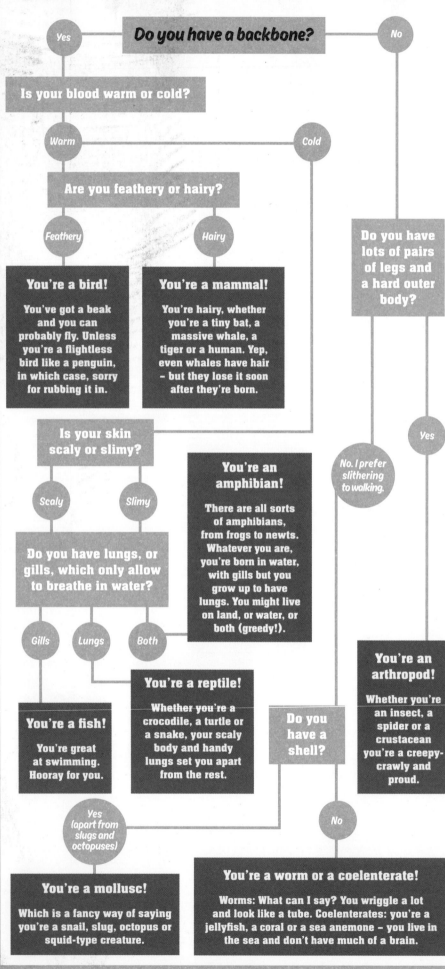

WHAT KIND OF ANIMAL ARE YOU?

Do you have a backbone?

Yes → **Is your blood warm or cold?**

No →

Warm / **Cold**

Warm → **Are you feathery or hairy?**

Feathery → **You're a bird!**
You've got a beak and you can probably fly. Unless you're a flightless bird like a penguin, in which case, sorry for rubbing it in.

Hairy → **You're a mammal!**
You're hairy, whether you're a tiny bat, a massive whale, a tiger or a human. Yep, even whales have hair – but they lose it soon after they're born.

Cold → **Is your skin scaly or slimy?**

You're an amphibian!
There are all sorts of amphibians, from frogs to newts. Whatever you are, you're born in water, with gills but you grow up to have lungs. You might live on land, or water, or both (greedy!).

Scaly / **Slimy** → **Do you have lungs, or gills, which only allow to breathe in water?**

Gills → **You're a fish!**
You're great at swimming. Hooray for you.

Lungs / **Both** → **You're a reptile!**
Whether you're a crocodile, a turtle or a snake, your scaly body and handy lungs set you apart from the rest.

Yes (apart from slugs and octopuses) → **You're a mollusc!**
Which is a fancy way of saying you're a snail, slug, octopus or squid-type creature.

No (backbone) → **Do you have lots of pairs of legs and a hard outer body?**

Yes → **You're an arthropod!**
Whether you're an insect, a spider or a crustacean you're a creepy-crawly and proud.

No. I prefer slithering to walking. → **Do you have a shell?**

No → **You're a worm or a coelenterate!**
Worms: What can I say? You wriggle a lot and look like a tube. Coelenterates: you're a jellyfish, a coral or a sea anemone – you live in the sea and don't have much of a brain.

FOR SALE

ONE BOWER Newly built. Includes shiny bottle tops, sweet wrappers and plastic straws. For sale because of lack of interest from ladies.

FRESHLY SHED SNAKE SKIN
Beautiful specimen from older snake who now only sheds twice a year. Lovely colours. Perfect for freaking out your friends.

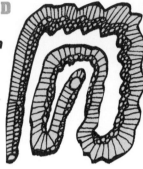

LARGE BADGERS' SETT
Situated in beautiful woodland near plenty of amenities including running stream and good supply of insects, grubs and frogs. Would suit fox or even weasel/stoat families looking to expand.

SINGING LESSONS
Larks: learn to sing while panicking AND flying! The secret's in the breathing! Cost: two worms a lesson.

LONELY ♡ ♡ ♡ ♡ HEARTS

MATURE SWAN, RECENTLY WIDOWED
Likes: preening, eating worms and long glides through peaceful rivers. Looking for a life partner. (Another one.)

NURSERY WEB SPIDER LOOKING FOR LURVE I'll bring you the most delightful offerings, wrapped up in my silk cocoon. Must have good sense of humour and NOT try to eat me.